CORNERSVILLE

The Best Place to Be

Written and Illustrated
by Reita Rea Hawthorne

Cornersville: The Best Place to Be
Written and Illustrated by Reita Rea Hawthorne

ISBN: 979-8-9861616-6-2

Roaring Lambs Publishing
17110 Dallas Pkwy Ste 260
Dallas, TX 75248

Phone: 972.380.0123
Email: info@RoaringLambs.org
   RoaringLambs.org

Ask the animals, and they will teach you;
the birds of the air, and they will tell you.
— Job 12:7 —

Table of Contents

Let Me Introduce You to Cornersville

1. The Jail—Sheriff Dandy Dan
2. Paramount Theatre—Pete & Pet Porcupine
3. The Rose Bakery—Rosemary Raccoon
4. S&S Flower Shop—Si & Sis Squirrel
5. The Stables—Fred Fox
6. Mr. Murphy's Grocery—Martin Marmot
7. The Raveling—Penny Possum
8. Dry Goods Store—Paw Possum
9. CNB Bank—Taylor Turkey
10. Rx & Sodas—Tim & Teeny Turtle
11. Courthouse—Mayor Baron Bunny
12. Dew Drop Inn—Cami Coyote
13. Morris' Jewelers—Morris Marmot
14. The Gazebo
15. Baseball Field
16. Cornersville Church—Pastor O'Malley

* Carly
* Cornersville

⑫ Murpheys Nursery

④ River Road to Cornersville →

N W E S

⑤ Cornersville Shortest route

Holly Glen Golf Club

②

⑦

Rhinestone River →

⑨ Woods and Wisteria

⑬ Roses

Misty Forest ⑥

③ Miz Maddie's Gate

①

⑭ RHINESTONE RIVER

Miz Maddie's Picket Fence ⑩

⑧ Platoro Reservoir ↓

Alberta Hill ⑪

Introduction

If you travel with me to Cornersville, you'll want to take a minute to study the maps in the front of this book. Then I'll introduce you to some of the townsfolk. Do you see Boss Bear Sr., as he stands in the Gazebo, welcoming everybody to the Founder's Day celebration? Now, listen to Martin Marmot read the Founder's Day proclamation, as he does every year, in his slow, deep voice:

"Cornersville has been our gift from the Land Grant of 1850, founded by the great grandparents of Cozy Coyote. Continually inhabited by the Caden Coyote family and joined in 1888 by the Brandon Bear family, Cornersville has become a thriving community of the kindest and warmest families in the entire state. Our town has been dedicated to hard work, high morals, and community spirit—guided by the rules of the Bible since its founding."

On the Fourth of July, you'll be in line for all the races and watch Boss Bear Jr. be dunked at the Dunkin' booth. You'll have corny dogs, fries, and sweets, and hopefully you'll be standing on a lucky number when Tina Turkey stops the music at the cake walk in the park.

As you run away Halloween night with Sissy Squirrel and her brothers, Seth and Sam, you'll be caught up in the mystery of the tall scarecrow. You'll thrill to the story of the little marmot, named Marney, long-lost from his family, when you see him carried safely up from the river by Fairy Fox.

You'll travel with Sheriff Dandy Dan and his six-man posse, made up of Bo, Baird, and Basie, the Badger brothers, Ritzy Raccoon, Cozy Coyote, and Fairy Fox, who ride in search of the stashed moneybags.

You'll swim with the Puddleduck gang, Daren and Denny, Daisy and Dixie. In the canoe episode, you'll hold on to your seats to see whether Buzzy Beaver and Teddy Turtle can save the boy scouts.

When everyone's all dressed up on Easter Sunday at Pastor O'Malley's church, you'll see frock coats and vests, shined shoes and new suits, picture hats and top hats, and more Easter bonnets than you've ever seen before.

You'll want to play baseball out in the field on the Fourth of July, and at Christmas, you'll want to make the once-a-year trip to the Orphan's Home in Carlyle. You'll pray for the friendly chicken snake Ziggy to have his voice back. And you'll want to listen to the stories praising *The Raveling*, the fabric store on the corner.

Let me start there. Find it on the map and I'll show you around. The Raveling—that's Penny Possum's store (the two ladies who help her are

Freda Fox and Sandy Squirrel). Paw, Penny's husband, owns The Dry Goods store next door. Next, you'll see Morris Jewelers, owned by Morris Marmot, and beside it on the corner sits the CNB bank with Taylor Turkey, president.

Now, move with me to the west of the square. There's Tim and Teeny's Rx & Soda shop. Baron Bunny's office is next door in the Court House. The eating place next door is reported as having the best lunch menu in town. It's Cami Coyote's Dew Drop In, with hamburgers, fried streak, potatoes, and greens—mainstays for folks eating downtown.

Across the way is the City Jail, where Sheriff Dandy Dan works. Next door is the Paramount theatre, happily run by Pete and Pet Porcupine. Next, The Rose bakery, run by Rosemary Raccoon, Ritzy's mom, assisted by his aunt Rosamund. It boasts the best homemade pies and cakes in town. On the north corner, sits the S & S flower shop, proprietors Si and Sis Squirrel. Most every event is covered by flowers from their store.

On the east corner of the square, you'll find The Stables, managed by Fairy Fox's dad, Fred. The rest of the block is given over to Mister Murphy's grocery, under the management of Martin Marmot, as is the Murphy nursery down the road a half mile.

You are all connected. Let's turn the page. There's someone special I want you to meet—Miz Maddie.

Miz Maddie, Matriarch of Cornersville

Cornersville, the Best Place to Be

Picture the white picket fence lining the sandy road, with huge old sycamore trees and hackberry bushes on either side. From the road, inside the picket fence, you see Miz Maddie's chicken house where she is raising her four girls, Minnie, Lucy, Jenny, and Annie, and her two boys, Brownie and Charley. While she isn't the oldest resident, Miz Maddie is the matriarch of Cornersville and all of Misty Forest beyond.

People there are all good neighbors, watching out for one another. There is no crime, maybe because folks are always giving you anything you need. Nobody wants to steal eggs, 'cause Miz Maddie is so happy to share hers. No one worries about twigs for a nest, because the Si Squirrel family is happy to gather enough sticks and grass for everyone. Barney Beaver and his family supply wood for standing structures. Mrs. Puddleduck offers feathers in case you want a soft mattress, and Ritzy

Raccoon and Boss Bear always bring enough of their fish catches to share.

Lest this picture of the good things in Cornersville paint a false image, I must share that sometimes dark shadows almost obscure the canvas. Shadows can foretell accidents or hover over bad choices. Like so many mornings, on this morning the sun is shining brightly, and the sunflowers are turning their heads.

All is well in Cornersville.

Everyone is so friendly. An hour ago, when Miz Maddie was out watering her roses and enjoying their fragrance, Zigzag Chicken Snake came scooting up the road beside her picket fence, tipping his straw hat with the black band and smiling at her, like he did to everyone he met on the road.

"Good morning, Ziggy," Miz Maddie said. "You headed to town?"

"Yes, ma'am."

"Be safe!"

Everyone affectionately calls him *Ziggy*. He is headed for the upper road into Cornersville. The junction is a half block up from Miz Maddie's place, where three weathered wooden signs stand tall on poles anchored in the dirt. One sign points to *Upper Road* to Cornersville, and a second signs points toward the more scenic but longer *River Road*, while the third sign leads to *Rhinestone River.* According to Miz Maddie, who never misses anyone going or coming down the road outside her yard, late at night Fairy Fox or Cozy Coyote travel the Rhinestone River road that winds down behind her house.

Any day would be an unusual day if folks didn't stop at Miz Maddie's gate to visit awhile. Yes, Cornersville is one wonderful place to call home.

By day the Lord commands his steadfast love; and at night
his song is with me, a prayer to the God of my life. — *Psalm 42:8*

"Look!"
Shouted
Jenny

The Swimming Lesson

"Top o' the morning to you all." Charley's cheery "cockle-doodle-doo" had everyone up on their toes very early.

"I know something you don't know," Jenny called over her shoulder as she ran out the door. "Here comes Mrs. Puddleduck with her four little ducklings."

Mrs. Puddleduck waddled right up to the white picket fence and looked at Miz Maddie's clan gathering to greet them.

"Oh, let's look at you," Miz Maddie clucked excitedly. "You look wonderful, and just look at your new little group. Please come in."

Mrs. Puddleduck rounded the gate, and her four little yellow fluff balls followed and stood happily in a line inside the yard.

"We're so glad you came by," Jenny said, closing the gate behind them. "Are you headed to the Rhinestone River?"

"Yes." Mrs. Puddleduck looked ever-so-proudly at her new family. "It's a perfect day to see if they can learn to swim. The sun is warm, and the river is low. Let me introduce them." She called each by name as she touched their heads with her wing. "This is Daisy, Dixie, Danny, and Daren.

"I think you know my children," Miz Maddie said, beaming. "But let me introduce my young'uns to your new arrivals." She introduced her girls Lucy, Minnie, Jennie, and Annie, and her boys Brownie and Charley.

Right that second, Miz Maddie's eye caught Brownie pecking at Daren's foot.

"Ouch, that hurts," the duckling squealed, looking over at his mother to see if she was going to do something about that chicken.

"Oh, my!" Miz Maddie lit into her offspring. "What in the world were you doing, Brownie? That's no way to treat a new friend."

"But Mama, look! He's joined between his toes."

"That's right," Mrs. Puddleduck said ever-so-sweetly to Brownie. "That's how they swim."

While Brownie and his siblings were staring at the newcomer's feet, Mrs. Puddleduck had a marvelous suggestion: "Why don't you come down to the river with us? We'll see if the ducklings' feet can serve as paddles."

And so they did. The chicken crew watched wide-eyed as Daisy, Dixie, Danny, and Daren confidently followed their mother between the reeds and down to the river's edge. On their first try at paddling behind their mother, they displayed amazing skills.

Mrs. Puddleduck was so very proud.

Back at the house, Brownie was distraught by the whole affair. "If chickens can't swim, what are they good for, anyway?" The weight of the world seemed to hang on his shoulders.

His mother kindly addressed the issue. "I know one thing you can be very happy about. Every summer, you are the only bunch in town that Mister Murphey counts on to save his lawn." She waited to see if they remembered. "Yes, every other week, he invites you to *bug-free* his lawn. You always have the best time, because he serves you marshmallows after you finish."

Brownie thought about that for a long time. In Mister Murphey's lawn, they always found lots of juicy bugs and grasshoppers. Then he turned triumphantly to Minnie, Lucy, Annie, Jenny, and Charley. "I'm glad to be a chicken, aren't you?"

"Yes, indeed," they said. And that ended the matter.

Happy is the man who finds wisdom. — Proverbs 3:13

Ritzy Raccoon

No morning in Cornersville had ever been prettier. The sun blinked its way through the cottonwoods as Minnie strutted down the river road to town. She had her Mama Maddie's basket on her arm, sent to pick up a yard of baby-blue fabric for her mother's latest project—a quilt for Penny Possum's little boy.

From the quilt shop, a honking horn caught her attention, and she looked across the street.

Ritzy Raccoon shouted, "Hey, baby. How 'bout a little spin in the Raceymobile?" The handsome convertible owner wheeled around and pulled up to the curb where Minnie was standing.

Minnie tried to look embarrassed.

"The way home won't seem as long if you ride with me." Ritzy Raccoon swung open the door and patted the seat where he wanted her to sit. "I'll have you there in a jiffy."

She couldn't resist. Besides, the sun was up a bit higher now, and the road home might be hot.

Along the way, Ritzy told her about a great place called the Avalon up on the highway. "Let's go there Saturday night. I can show you all my friends, and you'll see where everybody in town goes dancin'."

She didn't know what to think about that.

At home, she couldn't wait to tell her mother about Ritzy giving her a ride home. "And Mama, he asked me for a date. He was so polite."

"No, absolutely not. Ritzy is not the kind of boy you need to go out with. Do you know about the bad boys he runs around with?"

"Well, no," Minnie said, "but he was really kind today."

Miz Maddie was off to her sewing room. "That's all I'm going to say about it," she said.

Two weeks later, Minnie told her mother that she and some girls were going to the Disney movie at the Paramount. But she didn't tell the truth. Instead, she met Ritzy, and they drove to the Avalon, where three of Ritzy's friends met her at the door, their mouth's watering.

When they reached for her, she flew to the rafters and kept going up until she reached the highest perch, where she crouched in a dark corner. When her eyes adjusted to the dim light, she saw the open transom window and scrambled to it and flew down the roof. Half running and half flying, she scrambled across the grass straight for home.

She never looked up, but O'Malley Owl flew in and out of the trees behind her, just to be sure none of the Avalon gang caught up to her on her trail.

"Oh Mother, it was awful." Minnie sobbed as her mother tucked her in bed. "I'll never disobey you again. Please don't tell anyone what happened."

You need not worry, little reader, about O'Malley Owl. He would never tell. He kept the whole thing under his wing. After all, he was the preacher in Cornersville.

Children, obey your parents in the Lord, for this is right.
Honor your father and mother. — Ephesians 6:1–2

Aunt Rosamund

No need to go back inside. Ritzy Raccoon looked everywhere for Minnie. *She's probably home by now.*

When he pulled into the driveway, he saw his Aunt Rosamund sitting on the porch watching for the moonrise, as she often did.

She greeted him sweetly as he came up the steps. "For a Saturday night, you're home early, aren't you?"

He hoped he could bypass her and get inside before any discussion. "Yes, I have a science project that needs me tonight.

"Can it wait a few minutes? I want you to look at that moon. With all those clouds hovering, the moon looks like it is wearing a veil and lifting it up and down.

Ritzy turned to look. Sure enough, the night sky was a perfect picture, with the moon in a handsome frame.

She wanted to visit. "What's it like having a driver's license and a fine-looking car at fourteen?"

"Maybe not so good." He sat beside his Aunt Rosamund, his favorite relative. She had a sweet acceptance of his growing-up years, and always had a listening ear. "I really messed up tonight," he said. "I had a date with Minnie, Miz Maddie's youngest daughter, but she'll never speak to me again."

"Why it that?

"I wanted to show her what a fun place the Avalon is. When we walked in, three of my buddies surrounded us. They started fighting over who would get to dance with Minnie.

She didn't know any of them, and this scared her to death. She ran out. I ran outside after her, but she was gone. I'm sure she ran all the way back home."

"Did you ever think your 'buddies' aren't such good buddies? Maybe you should find some different friends."

As always, she was right. The other day, those guys wanted him to race. He was almost caught for speeding, just because he wanted their respect. He should be more careful.

Ritzy got up. "I do have some work to do—on myself. Thanks."

"Turning over a new leaf can take awhile, but with the Lord's direction, I know you can do it."

My son, keep sound wisdom and discretion;
let them not escape from your sight, and they will be
life for your soul and adornment for your neck.
— Proverbs 3:21–22

Cozy's Regret

For two years in a row, Cozy Coyote, by far the hero of the town, held the trophy from the Mars Mountain Triathlon. But on that hot August afternoon, this fine-looking fellow with thick golden hair was anything but somebody's hero. You see, the night before had been a long one, and the big celebration after his latest win had lasted until dawn. Food ran out long before the crowd did, and all he could think about was getting something to eat.

Near his house, he passed the familiar farm where Mrs. Puddleduck had built her nest in the bow of a weathered, gray rowboat. The boat's frame rested upside down on two sawhorses that had been built by Cozy's uncle over a decade ago.

If he just hadn't been so hungry, this next part would never have happened. Mrs. Puddleduck was back laying her eggs again. He spotted three big ones laying inside the old boat. Without thinking, he burrowed under the thick cassia bushes just inside her fence, grabbed the closest egg, and swallowed its contents.

Oh my, what have I done? Maybe she won't miss just one. But that one tasted so good.

He reached for a second one. Two cracked shells now lay on the ground at his feet.

I'll bury those back under the bush.

However, when he turned to see the one egg left in the nest, he couldn't stop himself. He ate the third egg too. He buried the last evidence alongside the other two.

Maybe she won't remember where she laid her eggs.

He looked to the right and to the left before he left Mrs. Puddleduck's yard. No one anywhere. Even if the case came to light, no one would suspect him.

After arriving home, he felt terrible.

What did I just do? I'm a thief. Those eggs were someone else's property. They were Mrs. Puddleduck's.

Since nothing like this ever happened in Cornersville, Mrs. Puddleduck knew she must report the missing eggs. Straight away the next morning, she went to the Sheriff's office.

Sheriff Dandy Dan waited until Mrs. Puddleduck quit crying over her lost eggs. The next minute, he was on the scene. He almost missed the evidence if he hadn't felt an indention right under his foot but saw something unusual. Holding his magnifying glass close to the ground, he found what must belong to one of the Coyote families. Cozy Coyote would never have been considered a suspect except for the strange configuration in the dirt—the footprint. Only one of that family had a missing pad on his left back foot: Cozy.

As soon as he saw Sheriff Dandy Dan coming up the road, Cozy knew he was in trouble. He confessed before Dandy said a word.

"Cozy," Sheriff Dan said, "what were you thinking? This sort of thing never happens in our town."

Cozy hung his head.

Had it not been for all the considerations of his past, the pleas and promises Cozy made to Mrs. Puddleduck, and the pressure Sheriff Dan received from the rest of the town to "let Cozy make restitution and give him another chance," he would have been hauled away to jail that morning.

After admitting the theft, Cozy went right over to Mrs. Puddleduck and apologized. He promised his "sorry" was the most sincere he had ever been.

Cozy lived up to his word. He rebuilt the part of the boat stern that had rotted and filled in the hole where he dug under the bushes. He did Mrs. Puddleduck's grocery shopping and any other errands when she or *any* of her family needed something from town. He was good as his word and became the most trusted citizen in Cornersville.

I delight to do your will, O my God;
Your law is within my heart. — Psalm 40:8 (NRSV)

The Baron's Legacy

Baron Bunny, for years the pharmacist in Cornersville, knew more than most doctors. As the senior resident in Cornersville, the old gentleman remembers when the railroad moved through the area at Petticoat Junction and how the townsfolk set their watches and clocks by the train whistles.

Miss Mousie, who had been his loyal assistant during those years, is now his housekeeper and watches over his needs.

Last year, Deary Deer, the principal, asked Baron if he would give a talk to the high school students on the history of Cornersville.

"Why, Mrs. Deer," Baron said in his deep voice. "It'd be my pleasure."

On the morning of the high school assembly, a heavy downpour fell, but all the students were in their seats, quietly sitting while the town's revered gentleman walked to the podium using his shiny black cane.

Miss Mousie watched proudly from behind a curtain to the left of the stage.

"Good morning," Baron Bunny said to the eager bunch of students before him. "I'll have question-and-answer time after I finish, so be thinking of questions you might have."

He said his grandparents had moved to this area at the turn of the century, in the middle of a grave drought, and lived through the Great Depression here. He spent the bulk of the time telling about a tragic event in the life of the small community. "You will want to remember, it's been over sixty years since the tornado hit downtown in Cornersville." The auditorium became so quiet you could hear a pencil drop.

"The Corner Drug Store, where I had worked forty-five years, flew up in the tornado. Bits and pieces of the store were strewn for ten blocks. That's where Mister Murphy's Grocery Store is today. The Lollipop Candy Store once sat on the corner of Main and 3rd Street, destroyed by the horrific winds. A year later, The Quilt Shop was built there. Two places I think may be your favorites, remained untouched: the Paramount Theatre with its great neon sign still in place, and Waltrip's Bakery. In the weeks following the tornado touching down, the Tire Store employees were still gathering their outside display of tires from blocks away.

"Some of you may have heard the story of the Cornersville Church dome. My father was standing inside the bakery when he saw the winds lift that heavy dome high into the air and then set it back in its original place. Amazing, don't you think?

"Just look at our downtown today. A really fine square with all the Cyprus trees lining the walkways and the park." He glanced at Mrs. Deer, who sat smiling.

A student's hand went up near the front of the auditorium which Baron immediately acknowledged. "Someone told us the courthouse has ghosts living in it, since the tornado."

"I don't know about ghosts taking residence in that historic place." Baron chuckled a bit, thinking about all the history the old building held. "I do know it houses the records of our town and the county. I think you'd be amazed how much information that building holds. From ancient land records and outlaws roaming the countryside, to every baby born in this town—they are all listed in those files in the basement. If you need information of any kind about this area, I think you'd be amazed. A lot has happened in this community since the courthouse was built in 1889."

When the bell rang in the hall, the kids stood to leave.

Baron waved. "Thank you, students. You were a good audience."

On the way back to the classroom, one of the students told her friend, "The Baron is a real wellspring of information, isn't he?"

"Yes, I'm excited," she said. "I'm going to ask my grandparents for their stories."

"Me too," another classmate said.

Call to me and I will answer you, and will tell you great and hidden things which you have not known. — Jeremiah 33:3

23

Nick

Ned

Acey

"Sachet Kitten

Acey's Bad Night at Black Rock

Acey and his two army recruit friends drank all the hot apple cider the armadillo boys could hold and won top prizes for Pin-the-Tail-on-the-Donkey, but they didn't want to stand in the long line to bob for apples. They wanted something more fun. Hot dogs wouldn't be served for another hour.

Acey had a great idea. "You guys haven't been to one of my favorite hangouts: Misty Forest. Wanna go? It's only half a mile."

"What's out there?" Ned said.

"Some of the best grubbing and the biggest bugs in this whole county. We'll have it all to ourselves. That's what."

They were all getting hungry. "Then let's go," his friends said.

And off they went. Soon, everything Acey had told Nick and Ned about the forest came true before their eyes—even better than they imagined. They moved in tandem, searching the vast pine-scented forest floor.

An hour later, Nick hollered up to where Acey and Ned were working. "Think we're missing the hot dogs?"

"We might be," Acey said. "Let's head back."

They had been so busy and excited, they never thought about anybody else being in the forest—until they turned to leave. There_was_ somebody else in forest! A small lady skunk.

"No!" Acey shrieked, thinking the skunk would listen. "Don't do it." He spoke too late.

When the three armadillo boys ran right into her path, Sachet Kitten was minding her own business in the forest.

"I didn't mean to," Sachet shouted. "Truly, I didn't. After the alarm goes off, I can't stop."

No one was there to listen. The boys were outta there.

"Gee whillakers," Nick said as they ran. "Where are we going?"

"Can't go back to the party," Ned said, hating his own smell.

"Stop!" Acey pointed the other way. "Let's go to the river."

All three raced behind Acey, stumbling and panting all the way to the river, where they plunged in, one behind the other. After continuous rubbing, splashing, and bobbing up and down, they didn't smell so bad.

They picked up a fast pace back to the party, hoping their clothes would dry as they went.

When they arrived, the band was playing loudly, and the Badger Brothers were singing "On Top of Old Smokey." Everyone was laughing, having fun, and you could smell the hot dogs.

The armadillo boys hoped to pass off their bad episode. But not a chance. When they approached the gazebo, everyone backed away.

Someone yelled, "Grab a hot dog or two and get some drinks, but go to the pavilion far away. You can still hear the music out there."

Yes, little reader. Indeed, it was a very bad night for Acey and his friends.

Let each of you look not to your own interests,
but to the interests of others. — Philippians 2:4

Teddy Confides in Miz Maddie

Miz Maddie Chicken was busy cutting away old blooms from her roses when Teddy Turtle appeared at her gate.

"Good morning, Teddy." She glanced up to greet him and then she sensed his anxiety. She got up off her knees and unlatched the gate. "Why don't you come on in and stay awhile?"

"Yes, ma'am, if you're not too busy."

While she held the gate, with each slow step into her yard Teddy slowly drug the dirt. "I'm here because you are the only one who might believe me. And I know you won't share what I want to tell you."

Hardly taking her eyes off Teddy, Miz Maddie latched the gate and headed for the swing. "Climb up here, Teddy. Let's visit awhile."

Miz Maddie patted the place in the newly repainted brown wooden swing. "What's this all about? I don't like to see you so nervous." She let

29

Teddy position himself before reaching over to pat his back. "We can work this out together."

He sighed and turned to face Miz Maddie. "It happened at the Halloween party last night. I was in the nursery, all by myself, very close to where the scarecrow stands."

"*What* happened?"

Teddy paused to take a deep breath. "Everyone else had just left to make a beeline back to the party, but you know how slow I am. I thought some of the kids were playing a trick on me. You know like a ventriloquist?"

"You heard voices?"

"Yes. No, I mean only *one* voice. The scarecrow's voice." Teddy's shell was shaking.

"Really?"

"Yes, he called my name and asked if I could keep a secret That's when I started moving away. I wanted to run, but I was frozen for a minute. When I could feel my legs, I raced away as fast as I could, cutting through the cedar break, back to town."

"That's really scary. Have you told anyone—like your mom or any of the kids?"

"No, ma'am. They wouldn't believe me. They'd be laughing forever if I told them."

"But *you* believe the scarecrow spoke, don't you?"

"Yes. After trying to get to sleep all night, I *know* he spoke to me. There was no one left in the nursery last night."

Miz Maddie wanted so much for Teddy to be in touch with what was real and what was not. "You go to the nursery often, don't you? He's never spoken to you before, has he?"

"No, he's never spoken to me before. And yes, I've been there by myself lots of times, standing very close to him."

"Maybe he only speaks on Halloween." She tried *not* to smile.

"Maybe," Teddy said, "I'll wait until next Halloween and go back when I'm not afraid."

"All right, that sounds like a plan. How about us making a plan. Shall we meet again, same time next year?"

"Yes, ma'am." He climbed down from the swing. "I feel better now. Thank you."

While he wasn't sure Miz Maddie believed his story, he knew she'd never share his story with anyone else. This would be their secret until after Teddy could check it out next Halloween.

He who goes about as a talebearer reveals secrets, but he who is trustworthy in spirit keeps a thing hidden. — *Proverbs 11:13*

31

Fairy Fox and the Missing Marmot Child

It was dark outside and not quite morning when Miz Maddie heard voices on the road outside her gate. She slipped out of bed and stepped to the front porch to listen and heard only the hoot of a faraway owl friend. She reached the fence, grabbed the pickets to steady herself, and squinted up and down the road. Only shadows from the trees full of wisteria vines moved in the wind. She opened the gate and bent down to look. There, a fresh track. She followed the outline with her fingers, feeling a dampness.

Fairy Fox?

Most every day, he had been traveling back and forth from the reservoir. Three months ago, he was the one who brought back the tragic news. The Platoro Reservoir dam had collapsed, carrying many away in the rushing water.

One of the survivors of that disaster, Mamie Marmot, came to live in Cornersville with her two children. Their granddaddy Martin Marmot, a quiet gentleman who lives alone up River Road, insisted they come. Before the tragedy, Mamie, her husband, and the three little ones lived happily among the rocks below the massive reservoir. But now they were only three. Mamie's husband and one of the children disappeared that night in the flood.

When they arrived, the entire Cornersville community welcomed them with groceries and home-cooked meals to help them settle in. Fairy Fox, who was one of the first to welcome Mamie and her children to town, said he would search for her husband and missing child.

Fairy was faithful to that promise traveling the twelve-mile journey day after day. Only last week, Fairy brought back from the river station a dark brown knit nightcap with a white ball on the top. The family recognized it. Daddy Marmot wouldn't be coming home. Where was the child?

Fairy Fox continued his search long after the emergency crews stopped their operations. He talked to everyone along the roads, asking questions. He posted signs, hoping someone had taken the *orphan* to live with them. He was determined to learn the truth so the family would know.

By the time the sun risen slightly above the trees the next morning, the news had spread across the entire community. *Fairy found the other little marmot and brought him safely home to his family.*

So now you know, little reader, the happy ending to the mysterious footprint in the road last night. It was Fairy Fox carrying the youngest marmot up from the river.

Little children, let us not love in word or speech
but in deed and truth. — 1 John 3:18

Almost Losing Ziggy

That night in Misty Forest, even if the moon had not been shining through the thick trees, Paw Possum would have spotted the friendly chicken snake Ziggy thrashing about on the pine-needled forest floor. "Ziggy, what's wrong?" he hollered. When he ran to his side, he saw the bulge in his throat, "You're choking." He grabbed Ziggy's throat with both hands, forcing the object out.

Something white fell into the leaves beside them.

Then Ziggy went limp.

Next thing you know, Paw had Ziggy wrapped around him as he ran toward the road behind Miz Maddie's house.

Miz Maddie was taking in the bedspread she had hung on the clothesline last night to air. The radio was reporting scattered showers, and she could already smell rain.

Paw yelled, "Miz Maddie, call Doc and tell him we're on our way. Ziggy's choked and gone limp."

She was on the phone quicker than rabbits can hop, and thankfully, Doc Deer answered.

"They're on their way," she shouted breathlessly. "They just left my back fence."

"Who's on their way?"

"Paw Possum's got Ziggy wrapped around his shoulders. He said Ziggy choked and is limp."

Before Paw ever got there, the office door flew open, and Doc Deer ran outside. "Bring him over here, Paw." Doc checked for a pulse. "He's unconscious, but he's still alive. What did you say happened?"

"I was on my way home when I found him writhing in the forest. I saw the big bulge in his throat. I used both hands to force it out. That's when he went limp."

Two rainy days later, Ziggy still remained in a coma.

Doc Deer asked everyone to pray, and they did. That first night, twenty of the townspeople gathered on the doctor's front porch in an all-night vigil. Others rotated the next two nights.

The third day, Ziggy woke up. He couldn't utter a word. Whatever had lodged in his throat had damaged his vocal cords. The townsfolk gathered around, and Paw was closest.

Doc turned to Paw and asked, "What do you think it was?"

"Don't know," Paw said, "but I'm going back to look for whatever might have caused Ziggy to lose his voice."

Back in the far side of Misty Forest, Paw looked for that *something*. He dug among briars, pine needles, and leaves, even turning over a damp log to see if something had slipped under it. He felt inside a short bush, and a small white ball fell out. "There it is!"

Paw hurried back to Doc's office with his evidence—a golf ball, for sure.

> *There are friends who pretend to be friends, but there is a friend who sticks closer that a brother.* — *Proverbs 18:24*

Acey Finds Boss Bear

at His Favorite Fishin' Spot

Boss Bear Steps In

That afternoon, if Acey Armadillo hadn't found Boss Bear down in his favorite fishing spot, he might never have gotten to the bottom of the terrible rumor. You see, yesterday the two Puddleduck boys had stepped outside The Rose, where they had been having lunch with some friends. They heard the crows talking on the highline wire about Ziggy the friendly chicken snake being a robber. Daren and Danny Puddleduck heard them say, "Ziggy got what he deserved for stealing eggs from Miz Maddie."

"Hey, down below." Acey crawled down the slope to where Boss Bear was leaning comfortably against an old oak near the water's edge. "How's it going?"

"Fine," he said in his deep voice. "It's always fine when I get to fish and the honeysuckle's in bloom." Chuckling, he said, "Even when it's

not, the fishing is always fine." He turned to watch Acey while keeping an eye on his cork at the end of the line from his bamboo pole. "What's happening with you? How's the family?"

"Everybody's doing well." He tried not to reveal his concern.

"How's Ziggy doing?" "That's what I need to talk to you about, Boss. He's doing well, "except the doc wants to keep him in the clinic a few more days. He hopes his voice comes back." Then Acey threw out his heavy-hearted question. "Do you know anyone who would start a rumor about Ziggy trying to steal Miz Maddie's eggs?"

"How did that get started?" Boss lowered his pole, tucked it under his leg, and faced Acey. "Was it because he choked on a golf ball, and Miz Maddie keeps those in her nesting boxes?"

"I guess so. Anyway, folks are wondering about that. Where could it have come from?"

"My goodness. I thought everyone knew where Ziggy was. Don't they know Paw Possum found him writhing on the far side of Misty Forest, next to the Hollyglen Golf Course?"

"I hoped so." Acey sighed sadly.

"Me and the Beaver brothers play there every Monday, you know." Boss pushed away from the tree and leaped to his feet "I've felt guilty from the beginning. Who knows how many balls we've overshot and lost to that forest."

"Really?" Acey's sadness turned to a smile. "That's the best news I could hear. It makes sense. But who would start such an awful rumor?"

Boss rolled his line around the pole and secured the hook and cork. "I know exactly who, and I'm leaving right now to track him down. I'll squeeze his bony neck until he confesses." With his pole and can of worms, he took off, the strap of his overalls loose and flying in the breeze. "Don't worry. As sure as my name's Boss Bear, we'll have this whole matter cleared up before bedtime."

Acey wanted so much to clear Ziggy's name. Poor thing—Ziggy couldn't even speak up for himself.

In Cornersville that afternoon, two young boys were feeling guilty for telling people what they heard the crows say, yesterday in town. They loved Ziggy, and now they had spread the rumor. They got to thinking, *Crows don't go into the forest, do they? Where did they get their information?*

Boss Bear had a good idea where the information came from, and he was after the culprit. That night in town, he hammered on the door of the jail.

When Sheriff Dandy Dan opened the door, there stood Boss Bear with his hand wrapped around the neck of a very battered Wiley Wolf.

"Put this one up for the night. Tomorrow, he has an apology to make to the people of this town—especially Ziggy. And he's now ready to confess, sheriff."

Little reader, that's how rumors get started. Someone hears something, and without checking it out, repeats the rumor as if it were true. Like a pebble cast into a lake, the ripples get bigger and bigger.

He who goes about spreading rumors reveals secrets; therefore,
do not associate with one who speaks foolishly. — Proverbs 20:19

Fire at the Paramount

The framed glass movie windows next to the theatre featured the coming attractions. Today, the big marquis overhead read—*Now Showing: Dumbo, the Flying Elephant.*

Everyone who could be there this first Saturday stood lined up on the sidewalk. Each one tightly holding the twelve cents in their hand, they eagerly anticipated seeing Miss Pet's face at the ticket window.

When the movie started, thirty-seven excited youngsters were snugly situated in their seats. Fairy Fox had Mrs. Possum's little boy, Patrick, with him. Also on his row, Cozy and Baird Badger, joined brothers Bo, Basie, and Ritzy Raccoon, plus the two Puddleduck girls, their brothers Daren and Danny, with Sissy Squirrel.

The rest of the Cornersville crowd filled the two rows behind them. There were all of Miz Maddie's group, plus Matt, Maci, and Marney Marmot, Seth and Sam Squirrel, and all of Cozy's sisters, plus Faith and Fanny Fox. Ritzy's sisters, Rena and Rae-Ann followed, and Tess and

Teddy Turtle came next, with Buzzy Beaver and his sisters, Beth and Betsy, right after them.

Up in the balcony, Pete Possum operated the reel, lights, and sound system. Halfway through the movie, a spark jumped from the movie projector and sparked the black curtains behind Pete.

The lights came on, and Pete yelled down to Pet, "Tell the kids to stand and line up. There's no need for alarm. Just lead them outside. There's been a spark."

Pet Porcupine, already on her feet, motioned everyone to stand and form a single line. She pointed to the exit door. "Walk slowly back up the aisle. Back row first. Go out to the sidewalk and wait for me."

They listened and did exactly what she said. But once outside, they all shouted, "The movie's on fire." Business owners, bank officials, and most all the folks on the square came running.

Pete had already doused the burned curtain and had the volunteer fire department there in less than five minutes. No danger.

Guess who the first responder was. Penny Possum. When she heard the kids yelling, she hobbled fast as lightning across the park. She was there before anyone from the shops near the Paramount, Fred from the stables, or Sheriff Dan arrived.

As soon as little Patrick saw his mom, he let go of Fairy's hand and ran to his mother's arms.

Listen to advice and accept instruction,
that you may gain wisdom for the future. — Proverbs 19:20

The Hawks

Easter Sunday Surprise

Seems everyone in Cornersville is arriving at church at the same time—except Ted and Teeny Turtle and their two, who came early to avoid being trampled. They sat on the second row, Teeny in her small yellow box-hat and Ted in his fine-looking blue-striped golf hat. Their little girl, Tess was all decked out in a pink bonnet and Teddy wore his clean white sailor hat.

Miz Maddie and her six came down the center aisle and took seats on the right side of the church, on the third row. Jenny, her oldest daughter, was wearing a beautiful violet picture hat with its neat bow tied under her chin. Miz Maddie's other three girls looked so smart in their pill box hats, one a deep red, another light green, and one blue. Paw and Penny Possum sat on the other end of the row. Penny had a petite royal-blue straw hat. Her baby Patrick was wearing a blue terrycloth sleeper.

Bim Beaver with his missus with their three teenagers were about to be seated in front of Miz Maddie. Al and Amy Armadillo, son Acey and his two friends, army recruits like himself, finished out that row.

Where were Boss Bear and his wife headed? Right behind Miz Maddie and her crew, on the aisle.

Granddaddy Marmot and his offspring chose to sit on row five. What pretty lacy hats Mamie and her two daughters were wearing. Her son was wearing a bow tie. How neat they looked together.

The other side of the church was filling up too, with Fairy Fox and his three cousins on the second row. Baron Bunny was farther down on the aisle, sitting by himself. Taylor Turkey and Tina were sitting right behind him. Ritzy Raccoon, along with his mom, dad, and sisters, joined their row.

Mrs. Puddleduck came with her four young-uns. Mrs. Puddleduck's beige picture hat was the showstopper this fine Easter morning. In their suits, her two boys looked so grown-up. Both her girls wore white organdy pinafores, tied in back, with matching white bows in their hair. Really sweet.

Now just look at the Coyote family coming down the aisle. Cozy was really something, sporting that black frock coat. He and his family—mom, dad, and six sisters—completely filled the fifth row on the far side.

All the girls had big picture hats. Anyone sitting behind them would have a hard time seeing Pastor O'Malley up in the pulpit. They were really decked out for Easter.

When the parade had slowed, one more Cornersville native came through the back door. For a full minute, Sachet Kitten stood at the back of the church, then sashayed slowly down the aisle with her fluffy black and white tail trailing like a royal train. She chose the very front row and carefully arranged her tail beside her.

A minute passed before Pastor O'Malley came to the pulpit and welcomed everyone. "It's wonderful to see all of you on this glorious Easter Sunday morning." He asked them to stand for singing the hymn "Christ the Lord is Risen Today." While they were standing, others came in and chose their seats in the back. When they began to sit down, someone turned to notice the new arrivals behind them. Deary Deer and Buck, as well as the Sid Squirrel family, had slipped in.

Folks gasped when they saw Henry and Hattie Hawk seated at the back. You couldn't miss them. Hattie had on a two-piece bright coral suit with a hat to match, and Henry was wearing a tuxedo.

Mrs. Puddleduck took a deep breath, happy indeed, that the Hawks were on the very back row on the *other* side of the church from where she was sitting. Up front, Miz Maddie cringed, as did Si Squirrel and his family when they realized they were sitting closest. Boss Bear, Acey, and others seemed undisturbed by the Hawks' presence. Some were remembering the loss of a family member to the appetites of the Hawk family.

Pastor O'Malley took an extra minute to adjust his glasses before beginning his sermon. "Today's message will be focus on Jesus' death and resurrection. Special attention will be given to the thief on the cross. Open your Bibles to Luke, Chapter 23, and follow along as I read verses 32 to 43."

Pastor O'Malley ended his sermon with a question. "Did you realize that the thief arrived in Heaven that day, with no merits of his own? He wasn't a believer until that moment, and Jesus offered him a place in Paradise." He went on to give the page number for the invitation hymn. "Will everyone please stand, and turn to page 120 in the hymnal. "We'll sing all four verses of "Just as I Am.""

Before they finished singing the first verse, something unbelievable happened in that little Cornersville church. From the back of the church, Henry and Hattie Hawk flew to the front of the sanctuary. All eyes followed their flight, and others took deep breaths when the pastor held out his hand. Next thing you know, they and the pastor were down on their knees beside the pulpit, crying.

When they stood back up, Pastor O'Malley turned to the congregation and shared the decision of the Hawk family. "Mr. and Mrs. Hawk have been saved today and are seeking church membership. Now . . . what is the feeling of the church regarding their decision? May I hear an amen?" After a moment, a whispered amen came from somewhere in the congregation.

"Welcome, friends," Pastor said, turning to Henry and Hattie Hawk. "Now, I know all our folks will want to come welcome you into our church."

Everyone seemed to be frozen in place. Finally, Miz Maddie stepped into the aisle and walked down to shake their hands. Ever so slowly, the others followed.

Never in the history of the Cornersville church had there been an Easter Sunday or any other Sunday like this one. A corner had truly been turned.

How good and pleasant it is
when brothers dwell in unity! — Psalm 133:1

Buzzy Beaver's Family to the Rescue

Two hours early, but Teddy Turtle couldn't wait. He wanted to get down to the water and stand on the dock for the first time, the place where he'd be spending a lot of time the next six weeks. Teddy had been named a Counsellor in Training (CIT) for Ryder Boy Scout Camp, as waterfront counsellor. He was so excited. In early June, he had completed his Junior Lifeguard course. Now, he was ready—more than ready.

The path to the water was sandy, surrounded by grass and plenty of rocks showing on either side. With the wind off the water blowing strong against his face, he didn't count the temperature as being hot.

As he stood there on the platform, looking down at the water, he felt like *King of the Mountain*, inhaling the river smells of algae and fish mixed with the pure aquifer springs. Early that morning, the military-style bugle reveille had sounded the wakeup call for Teddy and the twelve campers in his cabin. They dressed quickly and raced across two sandy gullies to meet the other campers gathering for the flag raising.

The flagpole stood on Camp Ryder's highest knoll, overlooking the river. Sunrise came just after the bugle's last note. Then, every camper and counsellor made a beeline to the mess hall for a bacon, egg, and biscuits-with-jelly kind of breakfast. What a great way to start the day.

Now, Teddy Turtle was alone at the pier, surveying the waterfront for twenty minutes, when something upriver caught his attention—a canoe with two occupants coming down the river. *What's a canoe doing down this far?* he wondered.

"Help," one of the occupants cried. The two screamed in unison, "Help!" Their canoe tipped and capsized, throwing both them and their paddles into the water.

Teddy was off the pier in an instant, paddling fast toward the overturned canoe. He reached the first boy, about eleven he guessed, and put him on his back. "Grab hold of both my sides."

Where was the other boy?

Teddy swam directly under the upside-down boat, wondering how he could manage a second non-swimmer. He saw something—two shapes in the water just ahead of him, and one was carrying away the other away, very fast.

Teddy couldn't overtake them, so he headed for the dock where he had been, now carrying the boy he had managed to save. He had no idea how much water this one managed to take in. As he pulled himself onto the landing and turned over his passenger, Buzzy Beaver appeared, pushing a second kid up on the board landing.

"Buzzy!" Teddy said, out of breath. "How did you get here? Did you see what happened?"

"Yes," Buzzy said. "Miss B, the girls, and I were on the other side of the river, cutting timber when we heard the screams. My dad yelled, 'Go, son.' I took one look, saw where the canoe toppled, and ran for the water's edge. When I made it made it past the middle of the river, I found this one. I looked for the second canoer, but now I see, you already have him."

The two friends exchanged big smiles, proud to be on the same team.

Two are better than one,
because they have a good reward for their toil.
— Ecclesiastes 4:9

Fourth of July

When Boss Bear's pickup rolled around the picket fence to Miz Maddie's house, the sun barely showed above the trees.

"Boss is here," Charley Chicken shouted, running back into the house. "Brownie? You got the freezer?"

"I'm coming," Brownie said.

The girls followed their brother excitedly as he carried the freezer to Boss, who stood holding the gate. You see, every Fourth of July morning, thoughtful Boss Bear stopped at each house to pick up wooden freezers so folks wouldn't have to carry them to the Town Square.

By nine o'clock, all kinds of excitement filled Main Street: ticket booths, the big Dunkin' booth reserved for Boss Bear, and booths for cotton candy, targets, hangman, and the corny-dogs—all spaced in the street in front of the theatre. In front of Mister Murphey's grocery, under the direction of Teddy Turtle, two of the Badger brothers, Bo and Basie, helped Seth and Sam Squirrel mark off the June Bug race, the three-legged race, the sack race, and the place for the watermelon seed spittin'.

At the corner across from the flower shop the home-made-pie exhibit stood under two heavily leafed pecan trees, where two men and one woman would name the first- second- and third-place winners. The raffle would be just before lunch, down by the gazebo.

Cozy came up to the gazebo driving the truck full of cracked ice so everyone could pack down their freezers. The sweet smell of mown grass filled the park. As dew lifted from the walkways, the warm dirt carried its own fragrance.

On the gazebo steps Mayor Baron Bunny paused to gaze proudly over his community. Flags fluttered in the summer breeze from every store. Red-white-and-blue sconces draped the banisters all around the square.

Inside the park, exciting areas emerged—bingo tables, horseshoe stakes, and washer boards, carefully positioned by Ritzy Raccoon, Cozy Coyote, and Bo Badger. The boys stacked the crates of Cokes next to the gazebo, donated by the Bear family.

At a nearby table, the Beaver girls were arranging washers, horseshoes, domino boxes, and the yellow burlap sacks donated by the Paw Possum family.

Not far from them, a table covered in white butcher paper held the tempting display of thirty homemade pies to be raffled mid-afternoon.

At ten o'clock the mayor checked his pocket watch, then signaled Taylor Turkey in the gazebo to lead the band in "Stars and Stripes Forever." The canon sounded. The Fourth of July celebration had begun.

Using a microphone, Baron Bunny's rich baritone voice welcomed everyone to "Our Forty-First Celebration." Then he read a portion of the Declaration of Independence, carefully pronouncing each word. "We hold these truths to be self-evident, that all men are created equal, that they are endowed by their Creator with certain unalienable Rights, that among these are Life, Liberty and the Pursuit of Happiness."

When the mayor turned to the flag, held by scoutmaster Coy Coyote, and placed his hand over his heart, everyone cheered. He turned to the crowd, "Join me in the Pledge of Allegiance."

The band struck up for the three Badger boys to lead everyone in singing, "America, America. God shed his grace on thee." When the song ended, Baron held out the microphone for Pastor O'Malley.

With his hat in his hands, the pastor spoke slowly and clearly. "Heavenly Father, please bless all our activities today, and keep us safe. Help us remember the words that we are one nation under God, for the

Bible tells us, Blessed is the nation whose God is the Lord. In the name of his son Jesus, we pray. Amen."

And all the people said, "Amen!"

By 10:30, cheers and screams from the Dunkin' booth alone filled the park. Everyone wanted a chance to throw the baseball at the target and cause Boss Bear to fall into the water. The screams increased when Tina Turkey's musical chair competition took off.

Teeny Turtle signaled the cake walk to begin. She played "She'll Be Comin' Roun' the Mountain" at high volume and created even greater noise when she lifted the needle and folks scrambled for their number.

Martin Marmot enjoyed the Fourth of July festivities more than anyone. Even though he was the owner/proprietor of the store and nursery that his uncle ran for years, Martin lived a lonely life. He and his sweetheart since grade school had celebrated their thirtieth wedding anniversary two days before she died.

Recently, the tragedy at Platoro Reservoir brought Martin's daughter Mamie and her three children to live with him. Today, watching them enjoying all the activities brought more excitement than he could remember, giving real peace to his life.

Basie Badger won the seed-spittin' contest. His brother Baird took second. Seth Squirrel's bug won the June bug race, with Mrs.

Puddleduck's boy Danny taking second place. Many an adult won a round at the bingo tables.

The only upset came when two of Ritzy's cousins came to take part in the activities. The town favorites, Miz Maddie's girls Lucy and Jenny, signed up for the three-legged race. Well, so did Ritzy's cousins. When Lucy reached for a yellow ribbon to tie her leg to her sister's right, Jenny felt someone push past them. "You don't need this one. We do!" The two Raccoon boys grabbed the yellow tie from Lucy. The only tie left was a blue one at the far end of the table. Stunned, the two sisters barely made it to the starting line when the race began. You can guess who won—the two Raccoon boys.

This broke the girl's winning streak, but they learned a valuable lesson. Life's not always fair. Their mother insisted they must not pout. They could still celebrate the washer competition, which their brothers won later that afternoon. And they did.

I have finished the race, I have kept the faith.
— 2 Timothy 4:7

Miz Maddie's Quilting Party

Tuesday morning at exactly one minute before nine o'clock, the first quilter arrived. Teeny Turtle tripped through Miz Maddie's gate and crossed the yard.

Coming in the door, Teeny said, "Your roses take my breath away."

Miz Maddie said, "Your blue polka-dot dress takes my breath away. With an apron to match."

Teeny proudly displayed her apron pocket, trimmed in lace. "I needed a place for my needle, thimble, thread, and hanky. See?"

Three more ladies arrived: Sarah Squirrel, her niece Sandy, and Mamie Marmot.

Sandy gasped as the she entered. "Your roses—do they always fill the air the way they do this morning?"

"Yes, they do. Every year." Miz Maddie looked out at the roses. "Maybe even more fragrance this summer. Ten years ago, I moved them from mother's house. You know, I think they have bloomed longer this summer."

"So lovely," Mamie sighed, staring out the window as Mrs. Puddleduck came into the room.

"Everyone's here." Miz Maddie clapped, then lowered the large wooden quilting frame from the living room ceiling. Five eager ladies sat down to admire it.

"You chose the perfect border," Sarah Squirrel said. "Just look how the navy-blue fabric shows off all the quilt squares." She lifted the corner of the backside. "And look at blue polka dot backing.

"Miz Maddie," Mamie Marmot said, "you've arranged our forty-eight squares into a masterpiece."

Almost in a whisper, Mrs. Puddleduck asked, "We're the first ones to see it, aren't we?"

"Yes, you are. Thank you so much for coming." She waited for everyone to take their seat. "I wonder how much we'll get done." She didn't wait for an answer. "Whenever we'd like to take a break, I have a pound cake and coffee in the kitchen." The aroma from Miz Maddie's cake made the morning even more special.

After every lady was busy stitching, the conversation turned to the town itself. Sandy Squirrel said, "I noticed how quiet it was in town this morning, with all the kids back in school."

Mrs. Puddleduck said, "It's quiet out our way too."

"If it weren't for Penny," Sandy said, "I wouldn't have a job. She's such a lovely person to work for."

Everyone agreed.

Mamie turned to look at Sandy. "You moved to Cornersville last year, just before school started. Yet you know most everybody in town, don't you?"

Sandy nodded. "Yes, one time or another, most everyone comes into the store. But I don't know *about* everyone in town. Keeping up with my kids all summer kept me a bit isolated."

"Who would you want to know about?" Miz Maddie said.

"I'd love to know about Penny and her husband—and her limp. Then there's the mayor, Baron. I wish I knew about Boss Bear's family."

Without looking up, Miz Maddie sweetly asked, "Will someone tell her about Baron Bunny?"

Tina Squirrel volunteered and told all she knew about the years Baron Bunny owned and ran the drug store. She even mentioned the tornado that took his store away. "Did you know he's the town historian? He keeps pictures and documents carefully filed of everything that's ever happened in Cornersville."

"Miz Maddie," Mrs. Puddleduck said, "tell her about Boss Bear's family. You know their story better than anyone."

"Oh, my! I've known that family since I was a little girl growing up here. I remember when Boss married Bess, and their first five years of marriage when they were childless. Such a happy day when Boss Bear Jr. came along. He was so cute." Miz Maddie let her needle rest on the quilt frame as she reminisced. "Both Boss and Beth had great expectations for "Little Boss," especially when they learned she could have no more children. They hoped he would be interested in the business world like his dad. But no, he had rather fish and help folks around Cornersville than bother himself with corporate responsibilities. Boss Sr. runs the S & D Wholesale Sundries business in Carlyle, twenty-five miles from here. He drives there from Cornersville, five days a week."

Not missing a stitch, Sarah Squirrel said, "You can be sure, without fail, that young Boss will be over at the Holly Glen Golf Club on Mondays, playing golf with the three Badger boys, Baird, Bo, and Basie. They say he's a really good golfer."

"If you cross those woods," Teeny Turtle said, "watch out for Wiley Wolf. He's turned some of the smaller members of our community into his dinner. It's not any secret that Wiley Wolf is usually up to no good."

Sandy quietly asked her aunt, Sarah Squirrel, if Penny's limp happened at birth.

"No," Sarah said, "two years ago, she and Paw were grubbing in the forest when a large tree limb broke off, fell on her hip, and crippled her. Lately, she seems to struggle more."

The conversation turned to Founder's Day on November 22.

"Two and a half months to finish the quilt," Teeny said, "and we can surprise Penny on Founder's Day."

With everyone filling their shifts, Miz Maddie said they'd surely have the quilt finished ahead of schedule. That was the plan, and everyone was in. The ladies took a fifteen-minute break and were back at work in record time. They didn't slow down one bit until quitting time at noon.

"Thanks so much, Miz Maddie," Sandy said from the yard as she was leaving. "It's has been such a fun morning."

Holding the screen door open, Miz Maddie hollered back. "Thanks so much for coming."

A cheerful heart is a good medicine. — Proverbs 17:22

Spelling Bee Test

Before school started in September, on a hot day in late August, seven students from Cornersville, plus three from Carlyle, gathered in high school Room 21 to take a written spelling test. The score would qualify them to compete in the District Spelling Bee in Sterling City. And *everyone* wanted to travel to Sterling City.

The Cornersville students included Marney Marmot, Rae-Ann Raccoon, Sam Squirrel, Cassie Coyote, Daren Puddleduck, and Miz Maddie's girls, Lucy and Annie

Instructions on the blackboard asked students to space themselves a desk apart throughout the room and have pencils sharpened. Open windows and wooden desks on black, wrought-iron legs lined the four aisles.

Promptly at nine o'clock that Saturday, administrator Bertie Bear Bertram entered the room hugging a manilla folder. She stood behind her desk a minute, smiling at the students, nodding approval at their seated spacing and bright faces. "Happy to see all of you here this morning. I will be handing out folders in a minute. You will use them to cover your work as well as insert your work when you are done." A minute later, she passed down the aisle, handing out folders containing 100 numbered spaces.

"I will be calling out each word three times. When I finish the last word, I will allow you five minutes to check your work. Let's begin.

"Assumption … Elegance … Certified … Delicious … Prioritize…"

Forty-five minutes passed. Each word had indeed been read three times.

"Now, take a minute to look over your work. When you are sure you have done your best, place your work inside the folder and lay it on my desk. I will be back to gather them."

The open window to Lucy's right let in a gust from outside. The wind blew the sheet Mrs. Bertram had secured under her folder on her desk onto the floor, landing sideways in front of Lucy's desk. On it were the test words.

No one else saw it, but Lucy did. She had struggled with the spelling of *pernicious*. During the summer, her parents, like most all their parents, had been going over and over spelling words. You could only take the test prior to entering the seventh grade in junior high. Now, the answer lay on the floor in front of her. *Drop my pencil, and stoop to where I can see the word. No!* the voice inside her said. *That's cheating.* She looked back at her paper one more time, carefully laid it inside the folder, and took it up to Mrs. Bertram's desk.

Out in the hall, Rae-Ann asked, "How did you do?"

"I hope I remembered them all." Deep inside her heart, Lucy knew she'd done her best, and she'd leave the rest.

> *He has showed you, O man, what is good; and what does the Lord*
> *require of you but to do justice, and to love kindness,*
> *and to walk humbly with your God.*
> — *Micah 6:8*

6 Miles to Mixon

Note posted beside the principal's office the past Monday:

Cassie Coyote, Miz Maddie's Lucy, Rae-Ann Raccoon, Daren Puddleduck, and Marney Mormot have qualified to enter the district Spelling Competition in Sterling City in November.

Cloudy and cool, but not too cool. Leaves falling in the wind along the sides of the highway. Today was the day.

Three excited girls jumped into the middle seat of the shiny wooden-sided station wagon.

Mrs. Deer opened the back so Daren and Marney could climb in.

"I'm so excited!" Cassie said, when Mrs. Deer started the engine. "I can't believe we're getting to go."

"I can't believe it's really gonna happen," Rae-Ann said. "There's five of us from Cornersville and two from Carlyle, who'll be there with all the other kids from across the state."

For thirty-six miles, the girls talked non-stop. Mrs. Deer and Bertie Bartram, in the front seat too. Meanwhile, Marney and Daren in the back were busy challenging each other in a handheld game.

Mrs. Deer hit the brakes. Their station wagon swerved to the left to miss the car ahead.

Three cars ahead steered off to the median, coming to a fill stop. The twenty-foot-wide median divided the traffic, giving their northbound traffic a separate stretch of road from the southbound traffic in the other direction.

"What happened?" Daren leaned past the girl's seat trying to peer through the windshield.

"A wreck," Mrs. Deer said.

"Oh, my!" Mrs. Bertram held her head between her hands.

"Look!" Marney said, "Cars are stopped behind us. Two men are getting out."

Two runners ran past their open car windows.

"Everyone, stay in your seats." After ten minutes, Mrs. Deer said, "We can all get out, but stand next to the station wagon."

What they could see was a torn-up car half on its side, mostly upside down, wheels in the air.

A man came back to report that indeed there'd been a one-car accident. The car had run off the road, hitting the median and flipping over once before taking two rolls on its side.

"The car has no doors on the passenger side," he said. "The man who was driving is standing outside the car talking to the lady huddled inside."

An ambulance siren blared from the opposite direction. It crossed the grassy median right behind them to get to the wreck. A red fire truck came from the same direction also crossed behind them. A wrecker arrived.

Daren asked, "Do you think the emergency vehicles came from Sterling City?"

The highway marker on the far side of the highway read, *Mixon 6, Sterling City 24.*

Mrs. Bertram nodded. We saw the overturned vehicle and its missing side doors. Items were strewn about outside the vehicle. Some white sheets of paper scattered in the wind. One blew almost to the tree across from where the Cornersville group was standing.

Lucy said, "Can I get it, Mrs. Deer? Maybe it's important."

Most everyone had gone back to their cars.

Before Lucy grabbed the paper from the shady spot, Marney said, "Look! There's two more, blowing your way."

Lucy gathered all three." These are pages from someone's Bible."

The firetruck left first. The ambulance pulled away. The wrecker removed the car. Ten more pages fluttered by. The chaperones watched the kids gather them, and everyone piled back into the car.

"Aren't we glad we left plenty of time to go to lunch before the competition?" Mrs. Deer said, turning the key to start up again. "You may have to gobble down those hamburgers from Martin's Kum Bak Place, but this won't keep us from being on time for the competition."

Lucy was busy sorting the pages in her hand. "These are from Genesis, and they are all in order through chapter thirty-six."

Rae-Ann said, "Do you think someone picked up the Bible?"

"I hope so," the ladies in front said.

"Could we find out the hospital where they took the lady," Lucy said. "We could take the pages there."

"Yes! Can we do that?" Cassie leaned over Mrs. Deer's shoulder.

"Here's what we'll do," Mrs. Deer said. "Mrs. Bertram and I will check the hospitals while you are in the competition. And we'll most certainly take them wherever she is."

Whatever you wish that men would do to you, do so to them.
— Matthew 7:12

♪ "The Lord's been good to me
And so I'll thank the Lord
For giving me the things I need.
The sun and the rain and the appleseed,
The Lord's been good to me." ♪

Ziggy's Surprise

It wasn't his birthday. But it seemed like it. Early in the morning, Ziggy wriggled all the way to Doc's front door. "Doc, it happened. I have my old voice back.'

"Ziggy! When?"

"Right after breakfast, I started singing my favorite song, the Johnny Appleseed one, and suddenly my voice wasn't raspy anymore."

Doc hugged the little guy and rushed to the phone on his desk. "Martin, this is Doc. I have some big news: Ziggy's got his voice back."

"Really? When?

"This morning."

"We need to have a celebration."

"How can we get everyone together?"

"I'll get hold of Miz Maddie. She'll get the ladies calling. We can have a party here at the store. How about noon today? I have plenty of Kool-Aid, cookies, and apples on hand."

Standing there in Doc's hallway, Ziggy stood wide-eyed with excitement

Twelve o'clock, and the Cornersville community turned out. The townsfolk crowded into Martin Marmot's Grocery, onto the sidewalk, and into the street. Wish you could have seen the extras that several ladies brought: one large angel food cake, pies, two plates of fudge, and additional plates of candies.

While shaking Ziggy's hand, Doc Deer silenced the eager crowd. "Can you imagine my surprise this morning when I heard Ziggy's voice on the other side of my door?"

"I couldn't wait to tell Doc," Ziggy said. "And I can't tell you how much I appreciate your prayers and the all-night vigils while I was unconscious. This is like my birthday. When I was in grade school here, I memorized what Alfred Lord Tennyson wrote, *More things are wrought by prayer than this world dreams of.*"

Martin put his arm around Ziggy and looked where Pastor Ollie and his wife Ombra were standing. "It's time to give thanks." And Pastor prayed.

Would you believe, before everyone left, Ziggy sang his favorite song for them? "The Lord's been good to me, and so I'll thank the Lord for giving me the things I need, the sun and the rain and the apple seed. The Lord's been good to me."

It is good to give thanks to the Lord, to sing praises to Thy name,
O Most High; to declare thy steadfast love in the morning,
and thy faithfulness by night. — Psalm 92:1–2

Sissy Squirrel

Teddie Turtle

The Halloween Escapade

Before they left the house, the two Squirrel boys, Seth and Sam, gave a clear warning to their little sister. "This is how it's gonna be tonight," Seth said, laying down the ground rules. "You can go to the party in the park with us, but you do your thing. We'll do ours. Don't try to hang with us all evening."

Hearing their admonition from the kitchen, their mother, Sarah, stopped washing dishes, dried her hands on her apron, and walked into the hallway. "Boys, listen to me. Sissy is your sister."

"We *know*," Sam said, "but she's always tagging along."

"Many people will be in the park tonight—those hosting the games and concessions and those coming to play. I don't want your sister to come up missing. Besides, it's going to be chilly out. There's a weather change in the forecast. Look out for your sister, will you?"

They nodded like obedient boys, but their hearts weren't in it. Later that night, the boys left the Halloween party, thinking they had put some distance between them and their little sister.

Halfway down the road to the Nursery, Seth said, "Don't look, but here she comes."

Seth turned and cupped his hands around his mouth. "Go back to the party. You can't come where we're going."

"No, I'm coming with you," Sissy Squirrel said, whining. "Mama said you had to watch out for me."

Seth pulled his brother close. Whispering, they hatched a plan. They waited until their sister caught up.

"Okay," Seth said, "here's the deal. We're going to Mister Murphey's nursery, and we'll let you go with us on one condition. You have to climb the scarecrow and read what's written on his shirt pocket." Whatever had been written there was almost covered by the scarecrow's overalls. No one standing on the ground could read it.

"Otherwise," Sam said, "you head on back."

With tears running down Sissy's face, she caught her breath and looked determined. "I'm coming," she said, hands on her hips.

The boys exchanged high-fives, thinking their sister couldn't be that brave. They ran ahead of her the rest of the way to the nursery. The mist was rising at this late hour and gave a spooky look to the already dark nursery. They strode boldly down the smoothly manicured sandy path and took their positions right in front of the Scarecrow.

"All right, go after it," the boys said, "*if* you're gonna stay with us."

A minute later, their mouths fell open when they saw their sister roll up her sleeves and stare at the big scarecrow. The next instant, she took a run and a big leap and scrambled up the scarecrow's denim overalls. She rested on his outstretched arm to catch her breath before she leaned out to read the words on his pocket. "Wizard of Noz," she said.

From *somewhere* in the night air, a voice said, "Sissy."

Scared to death after hearing her name, Sissy jumped the distance back to the ground and disappeared in the darkness, her brothers right behind her.

Teddy Turtle moved from his place in the shadows of the moon flowers bordering the pathway. Until now, he had been quietly observing the drama unfold before him, there in the garden. Leaving deep tracks in the sand, he moved toward the scarecrow. He had waited a year to learn what he now knew—the scarecrow could *speak*!

"Teddy, come around in front of me," the giant twelve-foot scarecrow said kindly. "I have something to tell you."

"You're talking tonight," Teddy said, challenging the statue. "Why haven't you talked the other times I've been here?" Teddy had returned to the nursery every week, hoping he'd hear the scarecrow.

"Because I am the Wizard of Noz, I can only speak on Halloween. I so badly wanted to talk to you last year, but you left."

"I know," Teddy said. "I thought I was hearing things, or maybe not. Either way, I was scared."

"I have a secret I want the whole town to know. You see, the blackbirds are my biggest nuisance. They are here every day of the week, trying to steal things. They have been carrying what I call the *Legend of the Scarecrows*. They cannot seem to devise a plan to retrieve the stolen money."

"What stolen money?"

"You remember the money from Mister Murphy's cash drawer was stolen three years ago, don't you?"

Teddy nodded. "One night, someone robbed the grocery and got away on horseback into the hills.

"You know he's dead, don't you?"

"Yes, he got killed trying to rob the bank in Sterling City."

"True, but he stashed the Cornersville cash in a rocky crevice not more than twelve miles from here."

"Really? Is it still there?"

"Yes, I know it's there. The blackbirds have said so."

"Do you know exactly where?"

"Listen carefully, the Wizard of Noz said. "The crows tried to dislodge the saddlebags. Too heavy. Too far down in the rocks for all their effort." The Wizard gave Teddy all the details for him to take to Sheriff Dan back in town.

After thanking the scarecrow, Teddy didn't waste a minute. In his fastest turtle run, he raced back to town, to carry the news to the sheriff's office, then straightway to tell Miz Maddie.

A wise man will hear and increase learning,
and a man of understanding will attain wise counsel.
— Proverbs 1:5 (NKJV)

Sheriff Dan's Posse

They weren't after a bandit, Sheriff Dan thought. Hardly a need to form a posse. We're only out to find the stash.

Since they *were* the posse three years earlier, the Badger boys insisted on a posse.

Sheriff Dan had a problem. He really needed only two or three deputies. He looked at the eager faces of those standing on the porch: Cozy Coyote, Ritzy Raccoon, Fairy Fox, the Puddleduck boys, and Miz Maddie's Brownie and Charley. He had an idea. *We'll decide by age.*

The Sheriff leaned against the porch railing and said, "Boys, there's no need to get in an uproar over all this. I'm only gonna take six with me. I have the Badger boys down already. I'm choosing by age, Fairy, Cozy, and Ritzy." He pointed toward the stables. "You six get a horse over there. Hopefully, we'll be back with the stolen money quicker than you can blink an eye."

At nine o'clock, they were off, raising dust along the main road. By 9:30, they were down River Road, headed toward Macon City. When they

came to the old railroad trestle, they stopped to follow the Wizard's instructions. Under the trestle, mud and grass greeted them. Deeper in, they met the outcroppings and the steep rise of the embankment. Two hundred yards beyond, they came to the chasm in the rocks, where the crows supposedly saw the thief hide the bag.

Sheriff Dan dismounted first and looked down into the hole. Sure enough, a saddlebag hung lodged between the sides of an even deep crevice in the rock formation. "Look, boys. It's here."

They gathered on either side and looked over his shoulders. Sure enough, it was down there.

"Bring the ice hook from my pack," Sheriff Dan said. "I've got the rope. Sounds easy, but the tedious, slow work lies ahead. Okay now, who wants to be first to try to grab it?"

Bo Badger was quicker than anybody else. Down on his belly, he leaned over the crevice and maneuvered the hook downward. No one spoke a word. This was risky business. "If the bag drops any lower," Bo said, "it'll be gone." After twenty minutes, he handed the rope and hook to the sheriff.

Now it was Sheriff Dan's turn. Trading places with Bo, he lay flat, resting on his elbows, trying to decide what would be his best plan. For thirty minutes, he kept trying to dislodge the stubborn leather bag.

Frustrated, he got back up on his knees. "I'll draw straws between the rest of you boys. The short straw tries next. Fair enough?"

Everyone agreed.

Cozy drew the shortest straw. Could he do better, sitting on the edge of the crevice, letting his heels rest on the other rim? He could lower the hook and pull the rope back through his legs. He fanned out his arms. "Now y'all stand back. Give me a little elbow room."

In less than fifteen minutes, he successfully hooked the middle piece of the saddlebag. Slowly, he pulled on the bag.

Everyone held their breath.

"Got it!" He pulled the bag out onto the grass and unhooked it.

All hands dived in to unbuckle the two sides. They had bills and coins to sort. When they finished, the content totaled $363.23. A mighty fine sum.

"Tie the bag here, behind my saddle, and let's go." Sheriff Dan mounted his horse.

With the bag tied securely behind his saddle, they sent dust flying all the way back to town, the Badger brothers in the lead.

Without a doubt, their dust cloud signaled everyone standing in the street near the sheriff's office. They guessed the outcome from all the hollering.

All the guys were yelling, "We found the money."
They had, indeed!

When there is no guidance, a people falls:
but in an abundance of counselors there is safety. — Proverbs 11:14

Baron Bunny

"Doc' Deer"

Si Squirrel

Coy Coyote

Taylor Turke

Fred Fox

Boss Bear, Sr.

Called Meeting of the Town Council

Mayor Baron Bunny called the meeting of the town council for 9:00 a.m. on Tuesday morning. The light from outside the window threw etchings across the wooden floor of the courthouse. The councilmen present were Boss Bear Sr., Taylor Turkey, Dr. Buck Deer, Coy Coyote, Fred Fox, and Si Squirrel.

While everyone excitedly came into the courthouse meeting room, the mayor stood and smiled until everyone was seated. "Gentlemen, as you know, we received news over the weekend about the money stolen almost three years ago from Mister Murphey's store. Thanks to Sheriff Dan and his posse, composed of Bo, Baird, and Basie Badger, Ritzy Raccoon, Fairy Fox, and Cozy Coyote, the stolen cash was located and retrieved about noon yesterday. I have it here before you on the table, a total amount of $363.23."

Everyone stood to clap and talk all at once among themselves.

"Okay, everyone be seated," the mayor said. "This is our good fortune. This morning, we must discuss the best use of our newfound treasure."

The floor was opened to suggestions.

Fred Fox's hand went up. "I think we should put a marker at the old Petticoat Junction to show people where the train ran for almost forty years." This seemed to be a very good suggestion. Petticoat Junction, two miles away, was once a thriving community, but the trains stopped coming, and the town vanished.

Next, the mayor recognized Coy Coyote, who said, "We've always talked about a swimming pool. Now that we have some money, we should build one."

Boss Bear stood up. "That is a good idea. We definitely need one." He paused. "But shouldn't we think about using the money to improve Main Street around the square with asphalt pavement?"

Doc Deer stood to give his preference. "Si and I have talked many times about the problem with the events in the park. We need to pour concrete around the gazebo area." The idea caught everyone's fancy because townspeople knew the picnic tables consistently went lopsided in the dirt whenever it rained. With the frequent events in the park, all Cornersville citizens would benefit from that.

"Any other suggestions?" The mayor waited, looking around the room. No hands were raised. "Are we ready to take a vote?"

After acknowledging everyone around the table, Boss Bear nodded. "Yes, we are, Mayor."

The vote was unanimous. As soon as they adjourned, the announcement would be made public. The crowd was eagerly waiting outside the courthouse to hear how Cornersville would benefit.

The multitudes with one accord gave heed to what was said.
— Acts 8:6

Baseball
Diamond

Chur

Founder's Day

What started off as a misty, moisty morning, turned into welcome sunshine for the ten o'clock launching of Founder's Day activities. The canon on the corner across from CNB bank gave the signal as blue windows formed in fluffy clouds overhead, letting the sun peek through.

All over the park, the breeze busied itself, launching lingering leaves. Tan ones, brown ones, gold and red ones seemed in a rush to finish decorating the ground. Only God could have painted the beautiful patchwork autumn picture for this Founder's Day, November 11, 1954.

The money from the robbery had been well-placed back into the ground. Most of the picnic area and walkways were covered in newly laid concrete around the gazebo. In his long black coat and white collar, Pastor O'Malley stood on the top step of the gazebo, holding his hat in his hands.

At full volume, the band played the Cornersville theme song. Everyone joined in singing, "This is our town. This is our town. Very best people anywhere around."

Baron Bunny stood next to Pastor O'Malley, watching all the people gather in the park, adding life to the colorful ground display. Two ladies were still working on decorations. Another pair hurried to set their picnic baskets on the tables.

At ten o'clock, Mayor Baron turned on the new handheld microphone. "A warm Cornersville welcome to all to all the mothers, dads, children, grandparents, relatives, and friends to this, our forty-first Founder's Day. Let's begin with prayer."

While the men and boys were removing their hats, Pastor O'Malley stepped forward. "Lord, thank you for this special day when we honor our heritage and your many gifts to us. Keep us safe, we pray. Bless our activities. In Jesus' name, amen."

The Baron turned to Martin Marmot, standing inside the gazebo, to come forward. "Will you read to these citizens our Founder's Day proclamation?"

In a clear, slow voice, Martin proudly read the proclamation. "Cornersville has been our gift from the Land Grant of 1850, founded by the great grandparents of Coy Coyote. Continually inhabited by the

Cayden Coyote family and joined in 1888 by the Brandon Bear family, Cornersville is a thriving community—a town full of the kindest and warmest families in all our fair state. Our town has been dedicated to hard work, high morals, and community spirit. Since its founding, Cornersville has been guided by the rules of the Bible."

When the applause subsided, the mayor called Taylor Turkey, chairman of the Town Council, to come to the front and make the formal announcement.

Taylor began in a cadence. "As you know, your city council enacted the decision to use the money recently recovered from the robbery of Mister Murphey's grocery store three years ago, in the amount of $363.23, to place concrete around the gazebo area."

The immediate applause was deafening.

"How does it look?"

Taylor waited for another round of clapping and shouting to end. "We are indebted to the effort of Teddy Turtle for listening to the scarecrow's message and sharing the instructions. We are grateful to Sheriff Dan and his posse, made up of Bo, Baird, and Basie, the Badger brothers, along with Ritzy Raccoon, Cozy Coyote, and Fairy Fox, for retrieving the stolen cash. Let's give them all a big hand."

Taylor had to hold up his hands to quiet the crowd. "We have another grand announcement. Will Miz Maddie, Sarah Squirrel, and Mrs. Puddleduck please come up to the gazebo?"

The three ladies fairly danced up the aisle. They were carrying what looked like a rolled-up rug, although many in the crowd knew better.

Miz Maddie took the microphone, looked over the crowd, and smiled sweetly. "Penny Possum, will you please join us up here?"

With the aid of her husband's arm, a surprised Penny rose from her chair and carefully stepped up to the platform.

Miz Maddie put her arm around her. "Penny, I'm speaking for everyone. The ladies of this town want to give you something. You've given so much to us over the years."

The crowd rose to their feet clapping, and the three ladies hugged Penny.

"Now," Miz Maddie said, "if you'll hold this corner, we want to show you something."

Maddie placed Penny's hand on one corner, and Sarah held onto the other, while Miz Maddie and Mrs. Puddleduck gently unrolled the quilt.

Ohs and ahs echoed across the park.

Penny was speechless. When she saw her name embroidered in the center of the quilt, she began to cry.

The three ladies told her she'd have time later to read all the names. Miz Maddie motioned for Paw Possum.

As Paw walked Penny back to her seat, many eyes in the audience filled with tears. Ladies searched for a hanky in their pockets or purse. Fairy Fox and Ritzy Raccoon stepped up to help the ladies reroll the beautiful quilt. In the background the band played "For She's Jolly Good Lady," with everyone singing at the top of their lungs.

When the canon sounded again, Mayor Baron said, "Let the festivities begin."

Many raced for the booths out in the square. Others waited till Coy had finished driving in the stakes for the game of horseshoes.

Over to the right, Buzzy and Basie set up chairs for the bingo tables. Paw, a really good caller, took his place in front of the large revolving metal basket that held the number cubes. Betsy Beaver and her mom, Miss B, joined Tina and her mom, Teeny, in handing out the beans and cards.

To the right of the gazebo, on the now-concreted area, two long tables covered with white butcher paper displayed fifty homemade cakes to be given away for the cakewalk.

"Come on, Minnie," Lucy Chicken told her sister. "We can be first in line."

A large circle was drawn on the ground behind the tempting table. Boss Bear marked off thirteen squares where feet could stand and move from one square to the next while the music played.

Folks formed a line for the cake walk while others took their seats for the first round of bingo. Some were eager to try the horseshoe and washer toss. Every activity cost ten cents—except for the cake walk, which was twenty cents. It all went for a good cause: the children's home in Carlyle, twenty-five miles away.

In her red-print apron, Tina Turkey ran to the record player, its cord carefully concealed so folks wouldn't trip. "Ready, everybody?"

"Yes!" everyone said.

She lifted the needle and started the music.

While "On Top of Old Smokey" played at full volume, folks moved around the circle from square to square. After a few rounds, Tina lifted the needle. She reached into a basket and drew a number. Guess who was standing on the lucky number and won the first cake.

"I can't believe I won," Paige Puddleduck said.

The young people, headed by Ritzy Raccoon and Baird Badger, busied themselves elsewhere, marking off a baseball diamond in the field behind Si and Sis Squirrel's flower shop. On the board beside the gazebo, the boys posted the announcement of the baseball game, scheduled right after lunch.

First game, Baird wrote in pencil. *Girls vs boys. Four innings. Girls are the Home team, batting at the bottom of the inning.* Below those lines, Ritzy scribbled, *After that, we'll choose mixed teams.*

Cozy had already arrived with the ice truck full of cracked ice for the wooden freezers. Some freezers held vanilla ice cream, a few with peach, and some were marked *surprise*. All stood ready.

The drifting smoke from the barbeque wagon, the latest addition for Cornersville celebrations, carried the beef and rib flavors through the fall air. Had it not been for everything else going on, a crowd would have lined up for lunch early.

On this day, an invisible memory had been etched in the newly laid concrete—a community of warmhearted folks who shared one another's lives and helped their neighbors, had laid a cornerstone.

You shall love the Lord, your God with all your heart, and with all your soul,
and with all your mind. . . . You shall love your neighbor as yourself.
— Matthew 22:37, 39

Sledding Down Alberta

Not twenty yards behind Miz Maddie's back fence was the perfect hill for sledding whenever Cornersville had a big snow.

At half past eight this morning, Miz Maddie saw Cozy Coyote at her gate, with two of the Badger boys pulling toboggans. When she opened the door and stepped onto the porch, the boys hollered, "Are Charlie and Brownie up yet?"

She didn't have time to turn around and call her boys.

Charlie and Brownie bounded out the door. "We're coming." While racing past their surprised mother on the porch, they pulled on their coats and ran to the barn for their sleds.

For the first time in four years, an overnight storm had covered Alberta Hill behind Miz Maddie's house with six inches of snow, making it the prime spot for sledding.

Miz Maddie yelled after the boys. "Pull your collars up, and keep your mufflers tight."

Cozy, Bo, and Basie waited with their toboggans until Charlie and Brownie came out the gate with their sleds. Their boots crunched through the snow as they trudged their way to the starting-off spot at the top of the Alberta Hill.

When Basie yelled, "Go!" the five boys pushed off to make the first tracks down the snow-laden slope. By the time they climbed back up for their second run, two of Miz Maddie's girls, Jenny and Lucy, were bravely skiing stripes across the slope, using their mother's curtain rods for skis.

On their second trip back up, Baird arrived with his toboggan, and Fairy Fox and Ritzy Raccoon came with sleds. As all eight boys lined up for take-off, Ritzy yelled to Seth and Sam, who were about to go down in innertubes. "What are you doing?"

"Just watch us," the Squirrel brothers said. Picking a spot alongside the others at the top of the hill, the races were on. At first, the toboggans led, then the sleds turn. The innertube duo proved their skills, circling back and forth down the slope.

Once everyone gathered back at the top, breathing white vapor. The Puddleduck boys stole the show when they arrived. They simply leaned on their webbed feet and flawlessly crisscrossed Alberta Hill in slow motion all the way to the bottom.

Their sisters, Daisy and Dixie, watched, then marched in their warm rain boots to the snowdrift and started rolling a ball of snow, which captured Sissy Squirrel's attention. Maci and Matt Marmot were soon helping them bring a large snowman to life.

An hour later some of the adults gathered: Mrs. Puddleduck, Mamie Marmot, and Rosemary Raccoon. Mrs. Puddleduck didn't last long before the cold running through her feathers sent her back inside Miz Maddie's warm house.

Before long, the kids had a real balcony crowd: Cami Coyote, Si and Sara Squirrel, Miz Maddie, and Penny and Paw Possum with little Patrick. They came just in time to see Teddy Turtle crawl his way to the starting point.

"Just watch me," Teddy said. He carefully tucked one foot at a time inside his big shell and posed, prima donna style, a second before he took off. You'd have thought he was on ice. Had there been a prize for the fastest descent, he would have won, hands down. Clapping and cheering, everyone told him so.

Boss Bear arrived on the scene just in time to see Teddy slide. He felt sure he too had a surprise in store. He carried a dull silver garbage can lid with a big handle. "Let me show you how it's done, boys." After pulling his red-and-white stocking cap down over his ears, he sat on the lid, grasped the handle, and took off.

Seth pointed up the hill from down below. "Here he comes."

"Oh, my. No!" Jenny shrieked.

Down, down, down he went, round and round, his hands locked into the handle, the white pom-pom on the end of his stocking cap in mad pursuit.

"He did it," Ritzy shouted.

Everyone crowded around Boss to congratulate him. The crowd at the top of the hill cheered loudest.

Just as he picked up his garbage lid, Boss caught a very strange sight out of the corner of his eye. He was quick to recognize someone rolling a tractor tire at the far end of the Alberta incline. "Look! Someone's climbing inside that tire!"

Indeed, *someone* was. Wiley Wolf came rolling down, inside the big black tire, making his own track in the snow in a smooth descent all the way to the bottom of the hill. Not everyone who watched the spectacle, hollered to acknowledge his success. You know, little reader, not everyone in Cornersville felt safe, getting too close to Wiley Wolf.

Boss, however, walked over to where Wiley had emerged from his tire. Clearly, Wiley had made a successful run down the hill in his unique means of transportation and achieved a real victory, unscathed. Cozy and Baird joined Boss in congratulating him.

When several of the boys offered rides to the girls, only Minnie was hesitant. Miz Maddie's youngest daughter had already taken off a glove to show she was through with the snow and the cold. She was going home.

"No," Fairy Fox said. "Don't go yet. You haven't had a ride down. Come on. One ride with me. I'll be careful, and I won't go fast."

Minnie stopped. "Will you go *real* slow. Do you promise not to tip me over?"

"Yes, yes," he said with the polite bow of a perfect gentleman. "I will go slow."

Minnie *loved* the ride. Problem was, when she grabbed hold around Fairy's waist and shoved both hands into his jacket pockets, she lost the blue-and-white mitten she had been holding. After Marney Marmot promised to go down the slope on foot and look for her mitten, she wiped away her tears.

It was almost 11:00 a.m. when Miz Maddie called from her yard. "If you kids want to come in and warm up a bit, there's hot chocolate and marshmallows waiting on the stove."

How exhausted they all were. Hot chocolate couldn't have sounded better. Up the hill they trudged to Miz Maddie's gate.

The little possum he sat up straight on Cozy Coyote's toboggan, smiling and laughing, as he was pulled up the hill to Miz Maddie's. Minnie jumped and shouted for joy when Marney came in with her missing mitten.

Do not withhold good from those to whom it is due,
when it is in your power to do it. — *Proverbs 3:27.*

115

Jail   Parament Theatre The Rose   S+S Flowers

Christmas Eve in Cornersville

Strands of tiny white lights blinked and sparkled from the giant Christmas tree in Town Square. Since early December multicolored lights had outlined storefronts across the square. Christmas carols played inside the shops.

Tonight was the Christmas time for the "Candle Lighting on the Square" in Cornersville.

Just after sundown, families began to arrive, all bundled up. Everyone was carrying a sand-filled sack. These were as much a part of Cornersville tradition as the star on top of the Christmas tree. Each sack of sand held a stocky candle anchored inside.

Youngsters and adults alike set their lighted lanterns in front of the shops and all down the steps leading up from the street. Cornersville had never looked more lovely.

The Beaver family was giving the town a special present—wooden silhouettes of the holy family—Mary, Joseph, and a manger with baby Jesus. Bim Beaver and his son Buzzy had carved the figures. Miss B and her daughters Benji and Betsy had given them a white sheen. Standing beside the gazebo, the silhouettes made everyone feel proud.

At seven o'clock, wearing his black overcoat and plaid muffler, Pastor O'Malley stepped to the center of the gazebo. He turned to face the gathering crowd. In his rich baritone voice, he began to slowly and carefully read the Christmas story from Luke 2. "And in those days a decree went out from Caesar Augustus . . ."

When he closed his Bible, all eyes moved to the three Badger boys standing out in the snow on his right. Bo, Baird and Basie sang, "O Holy Night . . . A quiet hush followed as they sang the final words, "O night divine."

Scattered snowflakes fell softly on everyone's coats and wraps. As the top of the gazebo railing turned white, the audience joined the trio in three carols. Well over a hundred voices, old and young ones, rang out in the cold night air with "O Come All Ye Faithful," "Hark the Herald Angels Sing," and "Silent Night."

Pastor O'Malley closed the service with a prayer of gratitude. "We thank you, Father, for sending your Son Jesus on this first Christmas, who is 'God with us.'"

The white fluffy stuff continued to fall, long after everyone had made their way home, quieting the night and covering the wooden silhouettes in a soft, warm blanket.

When the angels went away from them into heaven, the shepherds said
to one another, "Let us go over to Bethlehem and see this thing
that has happened which the Lord has made known to us.
— Luke 2:15

www.ingramcontent.com/pod-product-compliance
Lightning Source LLC
Chambersburg PA
CBHW080735250626
47170CB00010B/2844

* 9 7 9 8 9 8 6 1 6 1 6 6 2 *